Wake Up!

Katie Cleminson

Red Fox

For Bee and Bird

WAKE UP!
A RED FOX BOOK 978 1 849 41700 6

Published in Great Britain by Red Fox,
an imprint of Random House Children's Books
A Random House Group Company

This edition published 2010

3 5 7 9 10 8 6 4 2

RANDOM HOUSE CHILDREN'S BOOKS
61–63 Uxbridge Road, London W5 5SA

www.kidsatrandomhouse.co.uk

Addresses for companies within The Random House Group Limited can be found at:
www.randomhouse.co.uk/offices.htm

THE RANDOM HOUSE GROUP Limited Reg. No. 954009

A CIP catalogue record for this book is available from the British Library.

Printed and bound in China

Wake up . . .

and up,

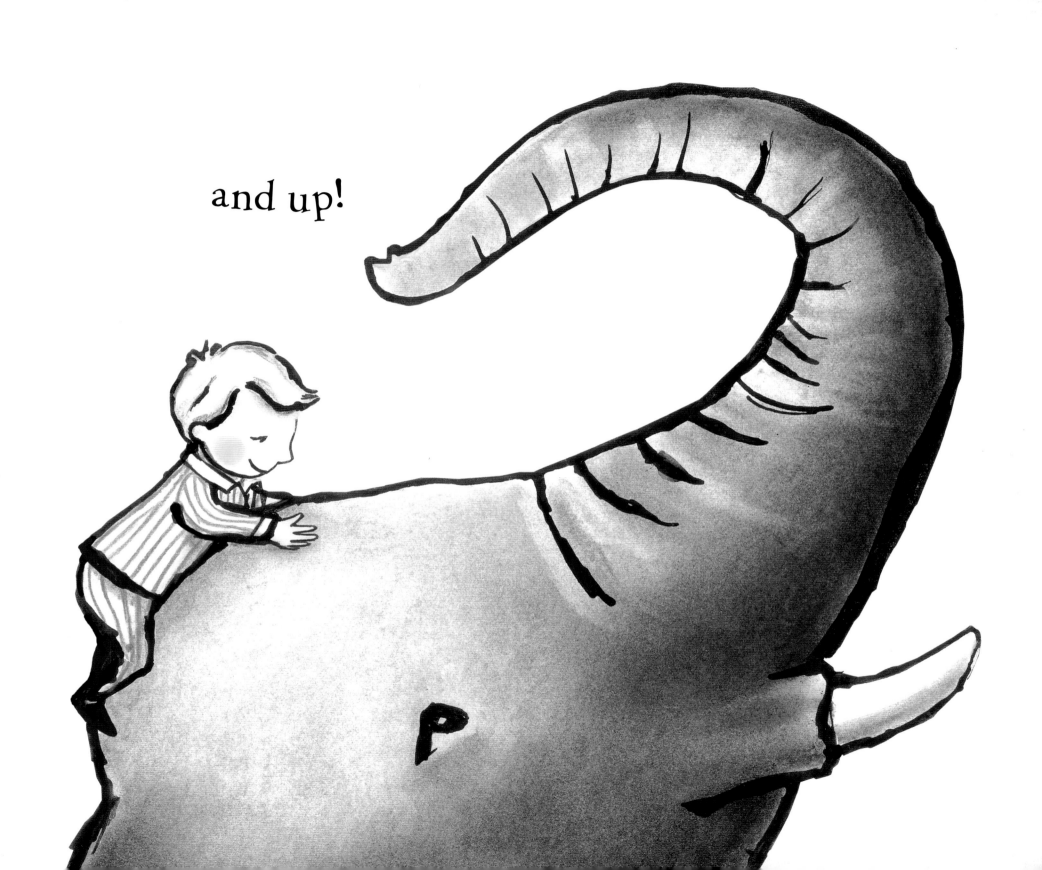

and up!

And stretch and scratch,

and scrub and wash,

comb your hair,

give teeth a brush.

It's time to dress.

Dress up . . . and up, and up!

Find pants and vests,

and shoes and socks,

and shorts and coats,
and favourite tops.

It's time for school.

Listen up . . .

and up, and up!

And read and draw,

and count and spell,

ask and answer,

show and tell.

It's time to play.

and up,

Swing up · · ·

and up!

And run and jump,   and climb and slide,

sing and dance,   seek and hide.

It's time for dinner.

Eat up . . . and up,

and up!

And chew and sip, and slurp and crunch,

use knife and fork,

and chomp and munch.

It's time to wash.

Clean up . . . and up, and up!

Then pick and choose,

and search and look,

and read aloud
the perfect book.

At last it's time to . . .

and up!

and up,

Cuddle up · · ·

Say goodnight,

yawn and stretch,

shut your eyes,

doze and rest . . .

It's time to dream . . .